For Real

*To Peg
Thanks for all the
Support over the years
And for being Real
Love to you,
Robin
♡ 2017*

SEASON Press LLC

Kalamazoo, Michigan

Copyright © 2017 by Robin Spiech

All rights reserved. No part of this publication may be reproduced, distributed, or transmitted in any form or by any means, including photocopying, recording, or other electronic or mechanical methods, without the prior
written permission of the publisher in writing to
robinstewartstudio@gmail.com

Published in collaboration with
Fortitude Graphic Design and Printing, and Season Press LLC.
Consultant Editor Sonya Bernard-Hollins
Cover art by Georgie Girl Images
Author photo by Holly West

For Real/Robin Stewart
Library of Congress Control Number
2017947601
p. cm.
ISBN 10: 0-9991334-3-8
ISBN 14: 978-0-9991334-3-9

Makenzie Hutchinson met Brinn in Kindergarten and felt she made a friend for life. When two boys moved next door to Makenzie, everything changed. Would their friendship last as Makenzie discovered a new love?

This is a work of fiction. Names, characters, businesses, places, events and incidents are either the products of the author's imagination or used in a fictitious manner. Any resemblance to actual persons, living or dead, or actual events is purely coincidental.

First Edition
10 9 8 7 6 5 4 3 2 1

Printed in the United States of America

*For Kayla, Ethan, Emma,
Mason and Hannah,*

Thank you for the laughter you bring into my life and for helping me see the world with fresh, inspired eyes.

RS

Table of Contents

Chapter 1- The Day My World Shifted   1

Chapter 2- Shake-Up, Wake-Up   15

Chapter 3- Fighter's Spirit   26

Chapter 4- Twists & Turns   32

Chapter 5- Strange Day   38

Chapter 6- Missing Oreo Flurries   45

Chapter 7- Wind in my Hair   54

For Real

ROBIN STEWART

Chapter 1
The Day My World Shifted

We met on our first day of school. She was hanging up her cool neon pink with lime green polka-dot backpack on a hook next to mine. My backpack was blue denim with only a tiny bit of silver stitching. Already nervous about starting school and making new friends, I now worried that mine was terribly ugly. There wasn't a chance in the world Mom would buy me a different one, though, especially since she had questioned my choice five times! I wished I had picked out one with a princess on it!

But, I decided it was best to take Mom's advice to put on a brave face, introduce myself, and say something nice to my new classmates. The girl standing next to me looked particularly friendly. Her brown hair was neatly clipped back with daisy barrettes that matched the daisies in her jumper.

I proudly looked at her and declared, "My name's Makenzie Hutchinson and I LOVE your backpack! Wish it was mine."

"My name is Brinn Landis, and I think *your* backpack is suuuper cool," she replied without hesitation. Then locking her arm around mine, she proceeded to drag me around the classroom jabbering about all the Learning Centers, and how fun recess would be. From that moment on, I don't remember a life without Brinn.

Our teacher, Mrs. Carlson, allowed us to choose one of the small gray desks with blue chairs that were arranged in blocks of four. We all searched out our claim and anxiously sat at our chosen throne.

Brinn leaned her face close to mine and whispered, "I hope that boy over there, sits over here." She pointed her tiny index finger with a neatly painted pink fingernail toward the bookshelves.

I stole a quick look over at "that boy" with pure curiosity. He was wearing blue shorts and a white T-shirt with a superhero on the front. He pushed his blond bangs out of his eyes and appeared to know a couple other boys because they were laughing about something. When two girls (neither of us knew) plunked down at the desks across from Brinn and me, Brinn just rolled her eyes and muttered, "Saaanks."

I would discover Brinn had a lot of made-up words that she expressed, mostly when she was irritated. I was already on to her when she mumbled in a hushed voice an extremely sarcastic, "Thanks, thanks a lot!" to the girls who dashed her hope of having the adoring Superhero boy sitting across from her.

Brinn possessed a certain charm, however, and everyone gravitated to her. That was a big perk for me. And everything and anything that Brinn liked, well…I liked it too.

***

The endless days of early elementary life were crammed with things like birthday parties, sleepovers and chasing boys around the playground. By third grade, there were also playground wars that ignited (mostly over a certain boy named Logan, who captivated us girls with his curly hair and dreamy blue eyes).

But without a doubt, I always had Brinn and my favorite pastime in the world—cheerleading! I kept a photo on my dresser of the two of us when we were six. That year, we had huge grins on our faces with hands on our hips, dressed in blue and white cheerleader outfits for Halloween. I was a cheerleader every Halloween from then on. Mom suggested other ideas like a cat, Dorothy from the *Wizard of Oz*, or even an evil princess. But I never aspired to be any of those.

When Brinn's mom enrolled her in the New Galaxy Gymnastics program, I was devastated that Mom clearly didn't realize I'd likely die if

I didn't get to join, too. Mom had numerous reasons why it wasn't a good time. She said it was expensive, she would rather I learn a musical instrument, and the clincher, it would be difficult to shuttle me around on the account of having two little sisters. I'd stomp off sulking, saying something wise like, "That's not my fault I have two little sisters! What about my life?"

I spent weeks wearing a scowl on my face, complete with daggers darting from my eyes. I suppose the phrase did truly apply to me when Mom commented one day, "If looks could kill, then I'd surely be a dead woman."

In spite of my bad attitude, Mom let me choose where I wanted to go for my ninth birthday dinner like she did every year. I chose Applebee's because their quesadillas were the best. As a special bonus, she let Brinn come along.

As we sat in our booth waiting for our server to come by so we could order dessert, Mom and Dad presented me with a card. I assumed some birthday money would be inside, which was fine with me because then I could pick something out at the mall over the weekend. It was one of those silly cards with a big-lipped monkey hanging off a tree branch.

As I opened the card Mom blurted, "Read it out loud!"

I sat up straight with the best nine-year-old posture I could muster and read: **"Congratulations on being 9 and a new member of Galaxy Gymnastics! Have fun!"**

Brinn and I squealed in gleeful unison. She jumped up out of her chair—first scurrying to my mom to offer a gigantic, Thank You hug—and then scrambled back to me. She threw her arms around me tightly and whispered in my ear, "I just knew she'd give in!"

We made such a ruckus that a few other patrons started to clap, and one guy hollered out, "You Rock!"

When the Applebee's staff came out carrying my birthday dessert, clapping, and singing an embarrassing birthday song, I noticed that some of the people at the tables around us sang along. Brinn leaned to me and whispered, "It's show time!" She then began to wave to everyone who watched and blew a few kisses from her hand out to the crowd.

I was always amazed at how she embraced awkward moments instead of wanting to run out the door and hide in the car.

***

Brinn was months ahead of me in gymnastics training and already moved up to the next level. I was determined to catch up with her and pushed myself to excel. When we were 10, our mom's realized how committed we were, and agreed to let us try out for the gym's Competitive Cheer program. New Galaxy Gym had a reputation for creating winning teams and we were ready to take on such an intensive challenge.

That season, Brinn made it onto the Starlight team and I landed a spot on the Star Gazers. I achieved the goal of making it into the same gymnastics training class with Brinn, but still aimed to win a spot on her competition team. We at least still traveled to cheer competitions together where we enthusiastically spurred each other on to "Nail It, Baby!"

***

The next year of my life, I experienced butterflies that raced in my stomach at cheer competitions, and I prayed I wouldn't puke during the dreaded tryouts. In the summer, when I was eleven, I cried all the way to the final tryout session and couldn't seem to stop.

Mom kept saying, "Just do your best," or "You're ready for this!" But when we pulled in the gym parking lot, her tone grew serious. "Look, you really need to pull yourself together!"

I was a panicky, nervous wreck as I envisioned

missing a landing or being out of sync with the other girls. I definitely had to work harder than Brinn—and most everyone else—but I was determined to step up my game. I needed to advance on to the next level and eventually cheer alongside Brinn.

Being a member of any cheer team required a lot of sacrifices though, like getting up early on Saturday mornings, practicing back flips and cartwheels every day during the competition season. It also meant having Mom tell me firmly, "No, I'm not buying that shirt, go put it back," all because she had been spending a lot of money on my uniforms, cheer bags, and hotel rooms.

Being on the team also had a magical kind of feel. I fit in and I couldn't imagine my life without it, or without Brinn. And truthfully, I wasn't good at anything else.

***

The summer before the seventh grade is when my life began to unravel. After an early morning sports physical at New Galaxy, Brinn and I came back to my house to practice our routines. I desperately was aware I needed extra practice time as I struggled to be consistent with my triple toe touches and back handsprings—and Brinn was always willing to help. Before we practiced, however, it was essential that we first glam-up in my bedroom.

Brinn shoved past me to beat me up the stairs to my room. She tossed her cheer bag onto my bed and flopped down next to it with her phone clasped firmly in her hand. She laughed so hard she made her infamous snorting sequence that grew louder and louder.

I had a hunch she was scrolling through her Instagram to post some unauthorized photo of me or someone from the gym on Snapchat. I grabbed the phone from her and confirmed my suspicion. There I was, all squinty-eyed with a pained expression on my face on a picture taken while I was stretching the day before at gymnastics.

"I have just one word for you, Brinn, KARMA! I'd be watching my back if I were you! Don't be surprised if your snorting pig laugh winds up on a Snapchat video!"

"Oh yeah? I'd like to see you try," Brinn laughed with a snort.

But, I didn't post things that would embarrass anyone, and she knew it. I quickly changed the subject.

"C'mon Brinn stay focused on me today!" I commanded. I was honestly struggling to get a new segment of the tryout cheer perfected. A strong pang of worry was creeping into my stomach and I confessed, "The try-outs are only four weeks away and I still look like a zoo animal! And you and I both know how bad that is!"

Brinn was well aware I was referring to the night of our Kindergarten Zoola-Palooza—a massively attended program for the entire county (or so it seemed). We were clearly amateurs. We just wanted to go home, but it was a kindergarten school tradition and there was an expectation to pull off the most professionally acclaimed performance possible.

Brinn's and my moment in the spotlight was ruined, however, when my lion mask slid off, only to reveal my horrified, five-year-old face. Then later on in the show, Brinn's striped zebra pants fell down, exposing her princess panties. The crowd was quite amused, but we were not. Let's just say from then on, whenever we experienced something horrific, we called it, "Zoola-Palooza Bad!"

"Kenzie, you're going to bring it, quit worrying about it!" She stated this with complete authority, too.

"But first things first, we have to get our game on!" Brinn scrounged through her bright orange cheer bag and pulled out a cosmetic bag full of eye shadow, blush, mascara, and several electrifying nail polish selections.

I snatched the bag from her and peered inside

to see the assorted pants and shirts she'd stuffed inside. I yanked out a small white shirt with the word LOVE scrawled across the front in big red letters.

"Does this really fit you? It looks like a baby shirt," I said with a hint of disgust since most of Brinn's clothes were smaller than mine. Brinn had a wardrobe that consisted mostly of skinny jeans and T-shirts that made her appear like a super model. She attracted plenty of attention. I'd noticed that lately a lot of the attention was from boys.

"Yes, it fits me, it's made of Spandex!" Brinn stated. She continued to view herself in the mirror over my dresser. She swirled her long wavy hair into a magnificent style that she called a pony bun. Whatever it was, she always looked stunning when she wore it. She ignored the fact I was a little envious of her.

"Will you PLEASE help me fix my hair like that?" I whined.

Brinn made a sad face in the mirror, "I've tried a million times Kenzie, but I just can't ever get it to look right."

I knew what she meant. I had straight thick brown hair and discovered that it simply didn't swirl like hers.

"Let's just put it in a side ponytail. That'll be cute," Brinn said in her happy tone.

"B-o-r-i-n-g." I spelled it out slowly for dramatic effect. But the truth was I hated spending an hour trying to arrange my hair anyway, so the side ponytail was actually fine.

Brinn placed the last bobby pin strategically in her hair then scooped up the photo frame from my dresser. "Awe, I love this pic of us, we're so sweet!" She held the photo next to her face and smiled in the mirror.

"You admire yourself in that pic every time you're here."

Brinn puckered her lips giving the photo a big kiss then twirled back toward me. "Whatever, I can't help it that WE'RE so C-U-T-E, cute!" she said unapologetically.

I secretly agreed. We were two adorably cute little girls.

"Time for some serious commotion right now, though!" Brinn shouted as she struck a pose with her arms as straight as possible against her body.

She was the perfect cheer model standing there in her yoga pants, pink crop top, cool hair, and mango-colored lips. There wasn't a doubt in my mind she'd be the cheer team captain and maintain her captainship all the way through high school. Then, she would land on the cheer squad for the University of Florida where she had already made up her mind that we were going together. We were going to be roommates, cheer partners, and BF's FOREVER. Most of the time I believed her. She was so certain about life.

While we waited for my Orange Tango nail polish to dry, I began to get totally jazzed up for our practice session until a reflection caught my eye out my bedroom window. I'd been waiting for the new neighbors to arrive since the SOLD sign went up weeks ago. "Yeah, Brinn, they're finally here."

I darted to the window with her right behind me. We watched a white SUV pull into the driveway. Right as it stopped moving, the back door opened and out tumbled a black dog followed by two boys. They looked our age, both had dark brown hair, wore faded jeans, and Chicago Bears team jerseys.

"Ooh la la," Brinn exclaimed in a sultry kind of way.

I hadn't imagined boys moving in next to me. I wasn't sure what to make of it. "We really need to get going," I said intently. But a weird chill sensation ran through my neck and arms before trailing down my back.

As Brinn and I gathered our scattered makeup from the floor, I glanced back out the window in time to see the older boy fully absorbed in kicking his soccer ball around the driveway with striking fancy moves. He didn't miss a beat. He

completed a quick spin and kicked the ball high into the air, caught it on the descent. Perfect.
Ooh la la, was all I could think.

***

Two days later, I decided to go to Brinn's house for our private cheer practice session, because the new boys had turned into one enormous, annoying distraction. I learned the older one's name was Nick, and the younger one, was Alex. I hadn't asked their names—I knew them because they constantly yelled to each other in the loudest voices possible!

If they weren't playing soccer in the backyard, they were shooting hoops in the driveway or throwing the neon green Frisbee for their dog and screaming, "Jump Blake, jump!" In the evenings, their father joined in the act, and until it was almost dark, they were whooping it up about some great shot. I did wonder if they even owned a TV? I wondered about a lot of things and found myself spying on them from my bedroom window or from the deck in my backyard.

The following morning I was awakened with a text message from Brinn:

BIG SALE. MUST GO! PICK YOU UP!

Mom, however, reminded me that I had

committed to watching my two sisters (Jessie, six, and Morgan, four) while she attended a Sales seminar. The regret bubbled up as I pondered why in the world I committed to doing this two weeks ago? I visualized Brinn finding the last rad hoodie and coolest funky bracelet.

As I complained to my mother, she unsympathetically reminded me again, "New jeans, shoes, and nail polish aren't free." And before she left, she went through her usual run down on how I'm supposed to do everything. I stood at attention and saluted her as she checked off her verbal list. When I witnessed her jaw shift to a crooked slant, I concluded that I was getting on her nerves a bit.

She finally cracked, "Makenzie Victoria Hutchinson, knock it off!"

At lunch, I contemplated letting Jess and Morgan just eat cupcakes. But Mom's words ran through my brain, "I'm counting on you." She always had to throw that in. So I decided to prepare a picnic to take out to the backyard.

I went the extra mile to make it as special as possible, too. I used a large heart cookie cutter to cut the bread slices, buttered them, loaded them with cheese, and made perfect grilled-heart sandwiches.

"TA DA!" I exclaimed as I tipped the plate toward Jess and Morgan so they could view my masterpieces.

They clapped and cheered with the approval of my sandwich savvy. I just really hoped to keep them fully occupied through lunch. Mom's August *Cosmopolitan* magazine had arrived in the mail and I only had a few hours to scour it entirely before I put it back in the mailbox before she returned.

I needed something to top off the sandwiches and prayed there'd be something in Mom's secret hiding spot in the back of the pantry. Jackpot! I discovered a family-sized bag of Cheetos—something we could usually only have at birthday parties or neighborhood barbecues. And as good fortune seemed to surround me, there was also some Hershey's syrup and a fresh gallon of milk in the fridge.

I poured the syrup in the large plastic cups and Morgan squealed with delight, "I want more chocolate!" She wrapped her arms around my waist adding, "I love you, Kenzie."

I thought to myself, *You are a remarkable big sister!* Even though I did have an ulterior motive. My sisters brought their slew of Barbies out with them and placed them in a circle on the blanket. Apparently, this was special picnic day for them as well. In that moment, my sisters seemed so adorable as they chattered away in their big girl Barbie voices.

I stretched out on my stomach and turned the pages of the magazine, studying each page in detail until the "distractions" came outside. They ran through their backyard like two dogs with their tails lit on fire. I could only shake my head in disbelief at how ridiculously loud they were.

Playing soccer, as usual, Alex eventually growled, "Good goin' stupid butt!"

I looked up to see the soccer ball sitting in Mom's rose bushes in the flowerbed that separated our backyards. I envisioned Mom's not-so-subtle reaction and muttered, "They better not trample those."

Alex noticed I was looking at him, so as he retrieved the ball he quickly offered, "Hey, sorry."

I replied in Mom's coy tone, "You don't have to be sorry for me, but just so you know my mom talks to those bushes like they are her babies."

"Thanks, good to know." His smile lit up his face. He spun back around and threw the ball to his brother before sprinting back to his yard. I couldn't stop my eyes from watching him.

Jess and Morgan half finished their lunches and rushed off to the swing set. I repositioned myself to re-engage in reading, "Seven Sure Ways to Get What You Want".

I was halfway into the article, when breaking my concentration was Alex's wild scream, "Watch out!"

This command coincided with a soccer ball careening from the sky, crashing into my chocolate milk, spilling the contents across the pages of the magazine, and splattering onto my face, arms, and my favorite white shorts. The ball continued its destructive journey as it knocked over the other cups and finally stopped on top of Jess's doll, Lily.

"Are you freakin' kidding me?" I said more like a statement than a question. I frantically wiped milk off the magazine. Jess, Morgan, Nick, and Alex just stood in front of me wondering if I would blow up, hit someone, or run off crying.

"Oops, oh crap!" Alex stammered as he looked down at the horrifying mess.

I glared at him in return. With Jess and Morgan staring at me I didn't dare say the words I wanted to scream. I knew they'd tell Mom for sure.

My sisters ran into the house for some paper towels. More than anything, I figured they didn't want to be around if I did blow my top.

While I surveyed the damage to the dolls, Nick picked up the magazine and held it up saying, "Geez, too bad about Christina."

The page was puckered with wetness and Christina's beautiful face now was covered with a huge chocolate milk stain.

Alex crouched down to collect the cups and

scattered Cheetos. "It really was an accident," he emphatically reported. He looked directly at me, but it wasn't remorse reflecting in his eyes. He was fighting a glinting kind of expression, and then a muffled sound escaped his mouth.

"Are you laughing?" I asked in complete astonishment.

"I can't help it. There's chocolate milk everywhere!" Alex said, still visibly holding himself back from busting his gut.

When I inspected my arms and my shorts I realized how ridiculous I looked. "Oh, I see how it is!" I tried to sound mature, but I actually stole this line from a Disney movie. "Well, maybe you better practice more on your pathetic excuse for kicking," I said, smirking at him. I was surprised I wasn't as angry as I had been a few seconds earlier.

His urge to laugh subsided. Instead, he helped himself to soggy Cheetos. "Mmm, love these things!"

Nick shouted, "Hey, I want some!" He found a couple still on the blanket, stuffed them into his mouth, and hastily licked the cheese off his fingers.

That's when I went into what seemed to be an out-of-body experience. "There's more in the house. I'll go change and get them if you want." *What? Did I just ask them to stick around?* I picked up the soccer ball and directed my gaze at Alex. "Just try keeping this in your own yard okay, Big Shot?" Then I dropped the ball toward my foot and booted it as hard as I could, which sent it sailing through the air and all the way over to the other side of their yard.

"Dang that was pretty sweet! Do you play soccer?" Alex asked slightly perplexed.

"No. I'm a cheerleader."

"Too bad! Maybe you should play soccer," he said matter-of-factly. "What's your name?"

"I'm Makenzie." I maintained a serious composure.

"Nice to meet you, Mak!" was his smart-aleck reply. "I'm Alex." He still had a glint in his eyes.

"I know! Whatever," I replied coolly. Nick interrupted our conversation to inquire of the bag of Cheetos in my house. Not looking at them I said, "Yeah, guess I could go get them." *I'm already in trouble, anyway.*

Jess and Morgan were on the deck clutching a wad of paper towels. I instructed them to start wiping off the dolls. And giving Alex and Nick my best-evil-eyed look possible said, "And they would be MORE than happy to help you!"

We stood around the swing-set for a few minutes as they devoured almost the entire bag of Cheetos in no time flat. Jess and Morgan provided most of the talking. But then, Alex announced he was going into seventh grade at Bayside—MY SCHOOL! I suddenly felt a certain panic. I was probably the first person he met from our school and hoped he wouldn't ask me to show him around on the first day.

"It's a pretty big school. I'm not sure I'll see you there," I stated, feeling it was important to establish this fact. But, once the words came out I could only think how stupid they sounded. Trying to change the subject, I turned toward Nick and asked, "And what grade are you in, stupid butt?"

Ugh, stupid again! My face felt hot, and I imagined it was turning bright red right before their eyes. I didn't know what to do next, so I squeaked out a goofy giggle-laugh in an attempt to prove I was comfortable calling kids I barely knew, "stupid butts".

Nick grabbed another handful of Cheetos and walked back through the flowerbed, "I'm going into eighth grade, Big Mak" (he had already given me a nickname). "Maybe I'll see you around?" He wasn't smiling just sort of grimacing.

"Maybe." That was the single word that came to me for a response.

I gathered all the sticky dolls and picked up the magazine. I closed my eyes for a second and wondered if Mom would notice that her August *Cosmopolitan* issue never arrived. *Yea, she probably would.* As I walked toward the house, I looked back at the two boys who were already conducting their business as usual. It was an eerie moment in time where I felt like my world was never going to be the same.

And I swear I felt the earth shift just a little.

Chapter 2
Shake-Up, Wake-Up

The next morning, I had to report to the kitchen before the sun was barely up. I was assigned the task of cleaning and reorganizing our humongous pantry after the unfortunate magazine fiasco. While sorting through the freaky quantities of soup cans, I heard Blake's familiar barking. I cleverly demised it was a perfect time to take out the trash (even though that wasn't on my list of things I needed to accomplish). Something gnawed at me to know what those boys were up to.

As soon as Alex spotted me on the deck he called out, "Hey Mak, come over and help us practice. We need another person."

"Nah, I don't like soccer," I shouted back.

"Well, have you ever tried it?

"Well, no, but I'm, umm, I just don't like it, that's all."

"How do you know you don't like it if you've never tried it?" he further questioned. "Oh come on, pretty please?" he said with a silly pout.

"Oh brother, what do I have to do?" I asked as I threw my arms upward toward the sky in a gesture to let them know I would save their day with my participation.

"Kick the ball, silly!" Alex replied.

Inwardly, I was bubbling with reluctance because I didn't always know what to say to boys. I spent most of my time with Brinn and the girls from gymnastics and Cheer team. But I trudged my way over to their yard as if I were being dragged by an unknown power.

I clearly communicated my stand, "Okay, but no crying like a baby if I hurt you. And I can't stay very long either. Because of you two stupid butts, I have a ton of extra work now!"

But they didn't seem to care about that. The boys were decked out like professional athletes in their multicolored jerseys two sizes too big. I figured they had dresser drawers over stuffed with crumpled up jerseys, shirts, and loads of mismatched socks—not to mention a heap of clothes on the floor.

Their backyard contained a massive regulation-sized goal net—a notable fact pointed out by Alex. Their dad completed it the day after they moved in as if it were of utmost importance. A pile of orange cones, a couple of Nike water bottles, and an enormous netted bag of soccer balls were positioned near the net. One thing was crystal clear; these goons were dead serious about their soccer!

Nick enthusiastically explained, "There's a freestyle competition coming up at the beach and club soccer starts soon, so we gotta dice it up"

I associated the word 'dice' with Dad chopping up vegetables in the kitchen. But surmised he meant it to be more like, "They were set on getting their soccer groove on".

"Yeah, ever since we moved, it's like we've lost our edge or something. We used to practice twice this much back in Oak Park," Nick said, a hint of sadness seeping through.

"Really? Oh." At first, I thought they were just messing with me since I knew for a fact they were out "practicing" since day one, hour one. But on second thought, I'd picked up my own practice pace lately as cheer try out routines were constantly playing on in my mind. "Yeah, okay. So, what do you need me here for?" I cut them a little slack.

"We need to practice receiving a pass from all different angles and challenging the goalie with stellar soccer moves. So, basically, we need you to start up by the house, dribble the ball down the yard, and boot it to me or Alex so we can charge the net for a goal."

He said it in the kind of tone that made me feel I'd better not let them down.

"Alex and I will trade off every three runs," he

added, sounding rather bossy.

"Well, first off, what do mean by 'dribbling'? And secondly, I want a turn challenging the goalie, too!"

"Oh, well, okay I guess. But you said you didn't like soccer. So anyway, dribbling is the term for kicking the ball down the field with your foot, maintaining control and not losing it to a defender. It's kinda' like in basketball where you dribble the ball down the court with your hand and then pass the ball off to your teammate."

"Yeah, you lost me with 'dribbling'. But I'll just run down the yard, kick the ball as I go, then kick it to you."

"You got it! THAT would be dribbling, and passing, AND assisting, if I make a goal," Nick instructed.

"Well, no one's making a goal on me!" Alex belted.

"Me neither!" Nick and I announced at the same time with conviction.

Alex and Nick swung their heads in my direction with the look of, "Oh, she is so toast." I didn't make eye contact, but a wild surge of fierceness built up inside me as I yanked the ball from Nick's hands, demanding, "Geez, let's just get on with it!"

I took on a resolve to prove to the new boys next door I didn't consider myself inferior. I was a legitimate athlete. I wasn't exactly sure why I felt this newfound intent to show off my capabilities, but I sprinted with stride and kicked an impressive on-point pass. When it was my turn to storm the next, I slammed a power kick that curved a bit as it swirled toward the net that resulted in a "Bam!"

"Man, you bend it like Beckham! Alex yelled.

"What's that supposed to mean?"

"You don't know David Beckham? The British soccer sensation? England World Cup champ? Epic tattoos? 'Bend it'? Alex stared at me like I was a complete idiot. The name sounded kind of familiar though.

"Wait a sec'. Isn't he that drop-dead-good-looking-hunky guy in magazines and on billboards who is, umm, well, wearing just underwear?" Alex rolled his eyes, turned around and walked away. I assumed his initial comment was still a compliment, though.

Yes, the cheerleader girl was a force to be reckoned with. That probably became most evident to Nick during the penalty shoot–out drill when he was the goalie. It purely wasn't on purpose, but I nailed the ball with all the muscle my cheer leg had, which sent the ball cruising and twisting through the air. It smacked Nick right in the private area boys protect at all cost.

"Cheap shot, Big Mak," Nick gasped, falling to

the ground. He dramatically rolled onto his back in the grass.

Alex thought it was pretty hilarious, and so did I, actually. But I wasn't sure what to say, so I said, "Oh, don't be such a wimp!"

Nick stood in slow motion, hunched over, and grunted, "Well, I'm done now."

"Well, me too. I have to go before you guys get me in trouble AGAIN!" I said, as I carefully maneuvered through Mom's flowers.

Nick hollered, "Still a cheap shot!"

"Whatever!" I turned to him and stuck out my tongue. There was something about him that just made me want to do it.

Mom met me at the patio door. "What are you doing out here? I've been calling for you all over the house."

"I took out the trash," I said, leaving out the added, "duh" part. Sometimes your gut tells you when you shouldn't push it.

She gave me the "Yeah, sure," expression.

Peeking through the kitchen window to see what the boys were up to next, I witnessed Alex's lips moving before he gave Nick a gnarly slug in the arm. *Oh, my gosh. These boys are so annoying!*

My phone was left lying on the counter. I couldn't believe I'd forgotten to bring it with me! Sure enough, there were four texts from Brinn asking what I was doing, and if my mom could drop me off early?

I text: **I WAS NEXT DOOR**

She replied: ***???!!!***

I went into double time arranging snack crackers, pretzel sticks, breakfast bars and cereal, then moved to the pasta, spaghetti sauce, and rice pilaf.

"WHA LA!" I announced when I finally completed.

Mom inspected each shelf as if I was becoming certified in Pantry Cleaning.

"Looks pretty good," she said, emphasizing there was room for improvement. Then she added the two-fingers-pointed-to-her-eyes gesture then, pointed her fingers back to me to signal that she was keeping an eye on me. I knew she meant it…at least at my house.

Brinn's two sisters were in high school, however, and we looked through their magazines, or we looked up things online with our phones or with Brinn's tablet. I think it was terribly hard for Mom to accept I was growing up. On most days, I didn't want to argue with her about these kinds of issues or plead for something I could mostly do elsewhere, anyway.

***

Brinn met me at her front door, insisting that I immediately divulge all my morning details.

She included firm instruction, "To NOT leave anything out!"

I filled her in; cringing through the part when I told her my, "Supersonic kick to Nick had sent my ball, well, in his …"

"Score for Kenzie!" she congratulated.

"It was an accident, I swear!"

"I thought those stupid boys annoy you to no end?"

"They do, I don't know, it's weird," I said, scrunching my nose.

"Well, you're a weirdo so I guess it's all good," she said flashing her facetious smile.

"Takes one to know one, I retorted," attempting my own version of a superior witty grin.

"Just don't let them distract you from your real mission—to make it on the Galaxy Comets All Star Team!"

Brinn's hints of disapproval for Alex and Nick was puzzling, especially since she'd had boys circling around her the past year. They never seemed to distract her from her gymnastic goals. I assured her she had nothing to worry about. To make it on the Galaxy Comets team and compete with Brinn was my biggest dream.

I advanced several levels at such a pace that most thought was exceptional. Brinn called me her "Shining Star friend". I called her "Ms. Coolio," on account she was extremely calm and collected under immense pressure, and well, she was stylishly cool.

Our daily life was centered on gymnastics. As we ramped up for the tryouts our total focus was on everything cheer. In fact, most of the girls were bursting with a peculiar type of mega energy that turned us into over-excited bundles of a-crazy-mess! I felt more like I was on a dangerously high roller coaster, in the car at the top just as it slips over the edge and your stomach feels like it's getting sucked out.

But Brinn was loyal and we practiced to the point of exhaustion. She forced me to improve on my weaknesses as if her very own life depended on me making it on her team. I mostly appreciated the strictness of her daunting coaching style. Sometimes I longed to lounge on the couch while watching reality TV and eating handfuls of potato chips. But I didn't reveal this kind of admission to Brinn, who would have undoubtedly questioned my commitment.

We'd diligently run through our drills at her house or mine before going to our gymnastics class. Brinn affirmed I was, "Spicing up my style, big time!" And her continual persistence was undeniably building up my confidence. But, the two weeks before tryouts were pure insanity.

First, Brinn's mom, Marla, dropped me off after our gym practice. There the boys were, in their driveway. Why did they have to be out front? Within a millisecond of closing the car door, Alex called out, "Hey, where've ya been?"

"Gymnastics, duh!"

"For like three days?"

"Every day, Alex. It's what I do."

I mean seriously did this kid think you rose to my level without working your fanny off?

"Holy crap! If you put that much time into soccer you could go pro."

I only had a second to think about his assessment before Nick broke into my thoughts.

"Oh yeah, we're supposed to ask you if you want to come to the Rowdies match with us tonight?"

I didn't even know what that was.

In Nick's further details, the Rowdies were a professional soccer team that played at Lang Stadium. And well, it turns out (at last minute) their mom couldn't go. They really didn't know anyone else to ask—that really added some charm to the whole invitation!

I was intrigued with being around the boys and had a surprising eagerness to investigate them further. I was somewhat, frazzled. My mind raced rapidly with what to answer before I heard myself say, "Okay. I'll ask my mom."

As soon as the words left my mouth, I dreaded the commitment. After all, I hadn't given it an ounce of serious consideration. I quickly plotted that I could make up some excuse or blame my mom for not letting me go. In further hasty contemplation, honestly, I wanted to tag along.

It would be one of the first times maybe ever, that I would be out on my own, without Brinn, the girls from cheer, or my family. I was blazing into new territory and my feelings were a mix of excitement and apprehension. I wasn't certain I'd like spending time with boys, but the curiosity persisted.

Anyway, I wasn't expecting Mom to grant permission to safari off with new neighbors. So far the communication consisted of Dad and Mr. Davis' exchanging of grilling techniques and discussing their jobs as they both prepared dinner in their backyards. And, Mom's front-door conversation with Mrs. Davis had only been when she dropped off a plate of chocolate delight brownies to welcome them to the neighborhood.

The deciding factor for Mom came when Mrs. Davis stopped over minutes later to offer the Mom-to-Mom kind of talk about kids and life. She gave the green-light assurance that all was going well between the new neighbor friends. The moms hit it off from the start—sometimes that's just how it is with certain people.

So, with her list of instructions etched into my brain, and my phone fully charged, she watched me leave for the game from the front door. It would turn out to be one of the most fun nights of my life!

The stadium lights beamed from miles away. As we drew closer, I felt giddy. Once inside, I was surrounded by a crowd of mostly men and boys who were ready to spur on their team with an enthusiasm that was contagious. The brothers were right in the mix, jumping around like two year olds; pushing each other every few seconds, and bickering about player stats. The fast-paced action on the field was enthralling. The crowd was fascinating. And the jumbo hot dogs were out of this world!

The boys felt they needed to conduct a play-by-play commentary like they were TV sports announcers. But, the game wasn't difficult to understand, and I hooted and hollered it up with the best of them. Brinn had always been amazed at my ability to project my voice louder than anyone she'd ever met.

Alex and Nick were blown away as well. I expressed it was, "A gift." I did apologize though, for the so-called "injury" to Alex's left eardrum.

Mr. Davis thought the three of us were "quite the clowns". But judging by how often he laughed out loud, I guess he enjoyed most of the shenanigans. It was obvious they were true-blue soccer fanatics at a proportion I'd never seen. I snapped some photos to capture the exhilarating mood, hoping the thrill of the night would linger in my mind. I loved captioning my photos with just a single word. These would read Food, Lights, Crowd, and Clowns.

On the ride home, we posted photos on our social sites and recounted the game. As a response to the Clowns photo of the three of us eating our jumbo dogs—complete with a big glob of ketchup on Alex's cheek, Brinn replied:

MOST ACCURATE!

The biggest surprise I didn't see coming, was when Nick spontaneously stated, "Alex and I are hosting a Backyard Soccer Boot Camp. It starts tomorrow morning at 8:30 a.m. And you, Makenzie Hutchinson are officially enrolled."

What? You can't enroll someone without asking! These boys were completely full of themselves! This was the message I was formulating to blast, but during my short pause, they already finagled me into agreeing to attend.

***

The boys astoundingly transformed their backyard into a soccer-themed course. On the far side of the yard was a long line of spaced-out cones, groups of balls were scattered at several places, and an exercise trampoline was near the patio. The boys were in progress of conducting dazzling maneuvers, kicking the ball with one foot to the other with impressive precision. A vision of them some day playing for the Rowdies suddenly didn't seem off base.

"Hey there, Makenzie Hutchinson reporting for duty SIRS!" I announced.

Nick held his fist up and shouted, "Hoorah!"

"I see we have a Boot Camp mascot," I nodded toward Blake who was lying near his kiddie pool with a small ball between his front paws. He was wearing a bright blue Adidas bandana around his neck.

"Ha, ha, yeah," said Alex, bending over to pick up a folder from the ground. "Here's some soccer terms and rules for you to learn. And there will be a quiz!"

"Um, I'm not taking any quiz–this is summer vacation!"

"Well then you won't be awarded this classy completion pin," he replied, holding up a pin with a soccer ball on it.

"This one's from a tournament back when I played AYSO soccer. Hmm, I think I was 6."

"I'll think about it." I said, trying to decide if this "camp" was worth all this effort.

Alex took the first page from my folder. "This is today's drill itinerary."

I scanned the page that had headings in bold with brief descriptions. "So, today it says I'm working on skills like dribbling, juggling, spot kicking, and step overs. And hey, why does it say on the Bicycle Kick, "Not Mak?"

Nick's exaggerated snicker was followed by: "Well if you think you're up to speed before you even begin, and can peddle both legs in the air and kick the ball backward over your head, go for it!" At this point, he started in uncontrollable laughter. "Mak, you crack me up! Alex and I can't even pull off that move. Not yet, anyway!"

Alex joined in. And although I normally don't like it when anyone laughs at me, I let out a squeaky sound, close to a real laugh, that I hoped they hadn't noticed.

We continued on where I learned sleek techniques for landing the ball in the goal and how to "kick with a vengeance", as they liked to call it. The juggling drill was the attempt to conduct as many consecutive mini kicks we could do standing, stationary, and kicking the ball slightly in the air. Although at first, I was unsure I'd hold the proper balance, I caught on quickly and accomplished thirteen on my third attempt. Not too shabby for a rookie.

Alex claimed, 'You must already secretly be in a soccer club because there'd be no way someone who had absolutely NO prior experience, could learn techniques that fast!"

"Sorry", I winked and switched to my opposite foot. Before we moved to the corner kick drill, Alex inquired if I was beginning to like soccer? "It's just alright," I replied.

He proceeded to grip my shoulders from behind, and with a pretty good fake exasperated voice, said, "Man, I guess I'll just have to shake you to wake you, crazy girl!"

I didn't know how to respond, so I turned around and gave him a hearty shove which sent him to the ground. Shrugging my shoulders I gave him a toothy grin. "Oopsey."

He muttered something I couldn't make out as he shook his head quickly like when a dog gets out of the water. Oh well. I still wasn't sorry.

The brothers took turns as the team leader. They traded off to each other a referee whistle and clipboard that held performance checklists and stat charts. On Boot Camp day two, I asked when I could have a turn as a team leader.

Nick said, "As soon as you graduate, big Mak!"

"Well, when's that?"

"When you can beat me at a shoot-out without cheating!"

That was going to be like, never. It didn't discourage me. This new adventure was a blast. But I had no clue where it would lead. The new boys were defiantly shaking me up.

Chapter 3
Fighter's Spirit

My crazy schedule was wearing me down. There was the Davis Backyard Boot Camp in the morning, then practice time with Brinn in the afternoon. Gymnastics turned out to be super more demanding than I ever dreamed. Oh, and I didn't dare mention the boot camp to Brinn! If I had, she would have known why I was slipping during practice.

When I totally messed up on my back handspring sequence—that had been flawless for weeks—I painfully landed on my back in the middle of the routine. I was definitely off of my game.

Grabbing me up by the arm Brinn asked, "Where's your head today, girl?"

On the ride home, I had to confess my new activity; trying to keep a secret from Brinn was eating me up. So, saying a quick prayer to God for immediate, much-needed help, I took the leap.

"Um, Brinn, you know how I kept messing up today?"

"Yeeaah! You did seem to be in big-time La La Land."

"Well, it's just that...well, I'm in a soccer boot camp thingy with Alex and Nick. It's in the mornings in their backyard. And, um, and I have to get up early, really early, so we can do our soccer drills before it gets too hot. I'm just a little tired, that's all." I shared the information in a rush of monotone words with no pauses.

Brinn leaned in close to me, peering at me with squinty eyes. "Who are you and where have you taken Makenzie Hutchinson?"

We both laughed, but mine was the slightly nervous kind. The troubling feeling in my stomach was hard to describe. It was the type of churning you get when you're crazy excited about something but confused at the same time.

My life was not making a lot of sense to me at this point because I found myself thinking about soccer more and more. I loved how I felt when I was running. I loved learning how to control the ball with fancy footwork. I loved the outdoors!

"Maybe this new found 'passion' has to do with Alex and Nick?" Brinn suggested with raised eyebrows and noticeably judgmental tone.

But it didn't. She'd made it sound like I was in love with one or both of them. But I wasn't. I wasn't even sure I liked them all that much—although, I admit they did make me laugh. But there was something else nagging in my brain; something that Mr. Davis said one morning as he was leaving for work.

"That's an impressive natural soccer style there, Miss Hutchinson!" he called out. Then he held up his hand waiting for our high fives. "Keep pushing the pace. Ya gotta push the pace!" he repeated, as we all three slapped his hand with a spirited fervor.

There was a new side of me that Brinn didn't know about—no one did, not even me.

"Well, Mr. Davis told me I had some pretty impressive..." I began exposing my recent encounter.

"I hate soccer!" Brinn cut in before I could finish. Her words stung. I didn't know what to say, so I stared out the window watching the houses rush by. Staying quiet for any length of time was neither of our strengths, however, and she broke the silence with, "Hey, let's go to the mall tomorrow morning, I still need to get some jeans."

The only problem was, I already confirmed to Alex and Nick I'd be over to their house in the morning. Their Dad was going to run the boot camp because it was one of his rare free mornings. I'd developed the opinion that Mr. Davis was brilliant at coaching and I didn't want to miss out on his training time. Afterward, I had to baby sit my sisters, a sad reality of my life if I wanted any more new school clothes. I attempted to explain my prior commitments the best I could, but it was clear by her sullen face that she wasn't buying it.

"Let's go Sunday afternoon, then. I can wait that long, I guess," she said, not as cheery as usual.

I revealed a smile that reflected part goofy, part fearful when I sheepishly replied, "I can't."

Her expression changed to irritated. She crinkled her nose, stared her deep blue eyes directly into mine, and asked a bone chilling, "Why not?"

It was intimidating to spit it out, but she'd find out anyway. "I'm going with the Davises. They're taking me to a baseball game." A painfully quiet moment followed.

Brinn's eyes turned evil when she said methodically, "I can't believe this!"

Marla looked at us in the rearview mirror. I was positive she could feel the tension from the back seat rising up to the roof.

"What is it with you and these people? You just met them. You don't even like baseball."

That was true. I didn't care for baseball. But I hadn't ever been to a professional game, either.

"Or do you miraculously love baseball now, too?" Brinn said. There was coldness in her words.

Brinn's mom tried to rescue the day and offered, "Well, I think it sounds like fun, Makenzie. There will be LOTS of other days for shopping! Maybe next weekend?"

"Yes, that works!" I'd definitely make sure of it. But glancing at Brinn, there was no smile. She was looking at her phone. Neither of said anything for the rest of the drive.

She quietly muttered, "Ajay." It was a new made up word I'd never heard but assumed it was aimed at me. And I assumed its definition wasn't of a happy-go-lucky status.

I didn't want to have to explain. I shouldn't have to! When I got out of the car, I thanked Marla for the ride and said goodbye to Brinn.

She replied with a hasty, "Bye." That was all. No, "Have a great time," or, "Good Luck with Boot Camp." Or, "See ya on Monday."

I bee-lined straight to my room with my mind spinning. Was Brinn mad at me because I wanted to go to a baseball game? I contemplated texting her to tell her I was sorry. But I didn't know what to say I was sorry for. Somehow it didn't feel right to have to apologize for being me.

The next morning, I wearily dragged out of bed. It felt like I'd been at an eight-hour cheer practice. Every part of my body ached. I checked my phone. No text from Brinn. "Well, it's early," I whispered.

A few minutes later I decided to pretend nothing was wrong and texted her:

MORNIN' SUNSHINE

That's what I called her when we traveled to cheer competitions and had to get up at 5 a.m. Brinn wasn't a "morning person" so I enjoyed harassing her about it. She'd typically groan and moan like an old person, and grab a pillow to hide under grumbling, "Go away, annoying girl!"

While I was eating my Cheerios, my phone finally chirped a text alert:

MORNIN' ANNOYING GIRL

Whew! She wasn't mad. With my world back on track, my energy and happiness returned in force. Now, I was on point to crush it with the boys next door!

Mr. Davis had us warm up with a mile run around our neighborhood. It was one of those hot summer mornings that was all bright and steamy. The humidity quickly rose, causing our skin to feel damp and sticky the minute we stepped outside.

The boys were good at running, but so was I. My years of cheer had made me a lean, mean machine, and I had no problem keeping up. They were their usual selves, chattering about the horror movie they watched the night before, and what they should have for lunch—narrowing it down to cheese stuffed ravioli or pizza.

There was a pure magical feeling in the air like I was in the middle of a movie scene. Part of me wrapped my mind around that it was really happening. The other part of me had difficulty believing it was real at all.

A few short weeks ago, I never would've imagined that I'd be running a mile with two boys AND their dad! Or, that I would be learning about soccer and baseball, and listening to discussions about cars, dogs, cleats, Cheetos, ice cream, and dirty socks!

I pondered what my life would be like had I never met them. Then, I pondered what my life would be like now that I had. The pondering had to be put on hold though, because we launched into part two of boot camp.

When Mr. Davis ran the show, we had to pay attention and bring our best effort to each drill. That's just the way it was with him. Totally up to the challenge, I continually surprised myself with what I was able to accomplish with my determination.

At 10 a.m., Mr. Davis blew his whistle three times, "That's it for today. Fantastic effort! Way to bring it this morning!" Then he added, "You dudes are gonna have to start taking it easy on this ole' man!"

We knew he was just teasing. Mr. Davis acted like one of the pro players we'd seen at the stadium, and he effortlessly outperformed us on every drill. He wasn't even breathing hard. We, on the other hand, were breathing like we'd run a marathon. Our hair was all matted and stuck to our heads. We had huge smudges of dirt all over our legs and arms. At the same time, we were also completely charged-up!

Mr. Davis pushed all three of us incredibly hard in spite of the fact that this was only a backyard drill session. I wondered what it was like to be on one of his teams? Alex and Nick were lucky bums, but they probably didn't realize it.

As I was gathering my water bottle, phone, and new dreaded homework handout sheets, Mr. Davis said, "You sure do possess a fighter's spirit! You'll be able to tackle all kinds of pursuits in your life with that quality."

No one had ever told me that before.

Chapter 4
Twists & Turns

Sunday began with the huge dilemma of what to wear. This was my first Major League Baseball game! Several shorts, jeans, and shirts later, I decided on pink denim shorts with a light camisole and a hip white sleeveless top that zipped up the front. "A decent enough choice, I think," I remarked to myself.

Then came the next big dilemma. What on earth to do with my makeup? For cheer competitions, my teammates and I went all out with bright cheeks, deep dark lined eyes, sparkly eye shadow, and full lipstick smiles. But Mom's criteria otherwise was, "Just a smidgen of makeup is necessary."

As I stared at myself in the mirror, one of Mom's many sayings came to mind: "Sometimes less is really more." She occasionally did make a point. So, with a light Rose powder blush, some blue mascara, and a splash of cherry lip gloss, I told my reflection, "This is gonna' have to do."

But there were new concerns, like what I was going to talk about for six hours? I didn't know much about baseball except that it was really difficult to hit a ball that spins at a high rate of speed toward your face. And, that at three strikes, YOU'RE OUT! (Something I painfully learned in fifth-grade gym).

I was starting to drive myself a little crazy with all the fretting, so it was a welcome reprieve from crisis mode when Dad hollered up the stairs, "Breakfast is on the table, come and get it!"

And he did not disappoint. He served up an egg, bacon and cheese casserole that he was quite proud of, accompanied by his ultra fluffy Blueberry buttermilk pancakes. My sisters and I made it even more scrumptious when we smothered them in Blueberry syrup and loads of whip cream.

Then, Jess became a fun-mood killer. "How come I never get to go anywhere fun?" Then she did a loud, "Humph," scowled some more and continued griping, "I want to go to the baseball game! I want to go have fun. I don't want to stay here with Morgan! I want to …"

"Take a chill pill, Jess," I finally snapped.

"You take a chill pill!"

"No, you!"

"NO, YOU!"

"Girls, that's enough!" Mom said as she pierced her gaze at me with that look of, Really, Makenzie?

It was beyond my comprehension how a six year old could get on my very last nerve so quickly and easily. But, I did pause for a second to realize that some cool opportunities were flying my way, and the Davises were the ones to thank.

Aside from my cheer competitions, Dad wasn't an avid sports fan. But every year he did host a Super Bowl party at our house for his work team, where he served his award-worthy sausage and chicken gumbo with homemade Parmesan pita chips!

***

I doubt the day could've been more spectacular. As we arrived at Tropicana Stadium, Alex insisted I encounter the complete baseball experience. That turned out to begin at the food court concessions, where I was coaxed to order a soda in a Tampa Bay Rays souvenir cup, a chili-cheese dog, and a box of Cracker Jacks—a baseball tradition new to me. Thankfully, the Davis's insisted on paying for mine too, or I would've had to do with just soda and Jacks! Cha-Ching, for ball food.

We found our seats along with a group of spirited White Sox fans dressed in team shirts. Realizing that the outfit I'd chosen wasn't exactly baseball attire, I instinctively swiped the baseball cap from Alex's head and put it on my own.

"Hey, come on!" Alex fussed as he flung his hands at my head attempting to steal it back. But my startling-slick-gymnastic-karate-like moves proved successful, and he gave up. "Go get one of your own!"

"Well, I don't have an extra $25 in my back pocket, smarty pants," I smugly replied.

He probably had scores of hats, I justified. I liked wearing it. I felt like I fit in. When I excused myself to use the ladies room, I was pleasantly satisfied that it made me look more, "sporty".

At the sixth inning, it was time for the brothers' own baseball tradition: extreme nachos, minus the jalapenos. I didn't normally eat nachos, but the gooey, sticky cheese was incredible!

"I'll take some of those off your hands if you can't eat them all," Alex volunteered, showing off his cunning smile.

"Thanks for the offer. I'll DEFINITELY keep ya' in mind," I answered deviously.

Alex and Nick's chorus rendition of, "Take Me Out To The Ball Game" at the middle of the seventh inning was a heap of exaggerated ridiculousness. The off-key singing and wacky dance moves I guessed were mostly some scheme to embarrass me. But I wasn't fazed and joined in the nonsense. Although, there was mostly gibberish coming from my mouth since I didn't know the words.

I'm not positive what Mrs. Davis was thinking, but she was shaking her head slowly from side to side as if saying, "Oh, no, they've gone off the deep end." The baffling thing that most struck me, was I'd lived in Tampa since I was born but wound up rooting for the visiting Chicago team. It didn't seem odd. It felt right.

On the way home, Alex and Nick begged to stop for ice cream. Their mom responded, "Geesh, all you two do is eat!"

It was true. At this particular moment, they both craved an extra-large Peanut Butter sundae! It only took a few, "Please, please, PLEEASE!" pleads before the parents relented. I suggested my favorite place, Sweet Treats, which had a patio by the water. The staff was not only friendly but were masters at creating the BEST Oreo flurries. I was positive their menu had some outstanding peanut butter extravaganza.

I was right. The Peanut Butter Explosion included three scoops of peanut butter swirl ice cream, topped with hot fudge, a giant scoop of Reese's Pieces, a pile of swirly whipped cream sprinkled with chopped nuts, topped off with two cherries.

"That sounds so, sooo good!" Alex said like he hadn't had ice cream for a year. "You're getting one, right?"

"Uh, that would be a, no. I don't care for peanut butter."

"Who doesn't like Peanut Butter?" he seemed truly shocked.

I ordered my usual large Oreo Flurry. We sat in the refreshing breeze by the water replaying the events of the day and discussing major plays and favorite players.

"Mine is the pitcher!" I said, smiling.

"Go figure, that's every girl's favorite," Nick snorted.

At that moment I noticed that the sky exploded into magnificent cloud swirls of bright orange, red, and yellow. I pulled out my phone to snap a picture. *Gorgeous!*

I wasn't sure what I'd liked most about the day. I liked it all.

Mr. Davis threw in a 'curve ball', however, when on the drive home he said, "You know, Makenzie, you exhibit a real-deal talent for soccer. They have new teams starting up this fall in good youth programs just in case you're interested."

It took me a second to comprehend the information he'd just provided and why he shared it."

"Yeah, you'd probably be a superstar," Alex said.

My mind clamored for an intelligent response. I was taken back a little at being viewed as a potential superstar soccer player. I had wanted to be a cheerleader since kindergarten and had been working on improving all my cheer skills to make it on to the Comets.

"Oh, it's waaay too late for me to start soccer. The other kids have been playing since they were like, five years old." I sounded convincing.

"Some kids start at five, Makenzie, and some start at twelve. It's not too late, especially if you have natural ability. But…of course, it might require building up your faith in order to conquer your fear," Mr. Davis stated in his coach-kind-of-way.

Fear. That word. Yes, I carried some fear around with me about the All-Star team. But I finally felt I could compete at this new level. I had what it took to be there. It was comfortable. It was familiar. And most of all, it was Brinn's dream, too. We were in this dream together. I restated my position, "Competition Cheerleading is my passion. It's my life."

"Well, as riveting as competitive cheer is, it's simply not as cool as soccer," Alex scoffed.

He was purposely mocking me, so I punched him in the arm. I could tell by the glare from his eyes that my strength surprised him. Then, he pinched my bicep. I didn't know a pinch could hurt so much! It turned quickly to mayhem. I squealed, then, punched him.

Nick shouted, "You're a fat squirrel!" and punched Alex. Alex punched Nick, then, I pinched Alex. From the back seat, there was screaming, laughing, punching, pinching, and the dreaded grabbing of kneecaps that drew out my loudest protests.

"Okay, that's enough, someone's gonna' get hurt," their mom turned around and said in her not-kidding voice.

The rest of the way home we shared YouTube videos. The jokesters picked out all kinds of perilous sports clips or anything zany. Mines were music videos or cute animals. My mind wandered through the day's events: the game, the food, and the ice cream. I thought about the fact I didn't know how to pinch very well.

That night in bed, I wondered what the next day would be like now that boot camp officially was over. Would I go over to Alex and Nick's anyway? Then it hit me, I hadn't talked to Brinn all day! I checked my phone. No messages from her either. It was past my curfew for using my phone, but I couldn't let the day pass by without getting an update from her. It was worth the risk.

She reported the shopping was, "fabulous, fabulous, fabulous!" Brinn had an uncanny knack for finding unique clothes that she mixed and matched into incredible styles. Her sisters called it "snappy-chic", and all of us agreed that she should be a fashion designer. She had numerous sketchbooks of her ideas, which were simply... fabulous.

It brought relief to hear from Brinn. It was a perfect day and perfect night; the kind you wish they all could be. But before I drifted off to sleep, the happiness started to fade. The cheer tryouts were twelve days away, and something deep inside me was stirring.

I recalled what Mr. Davis said about building up my faith to conquer my fears. The only problem was, I wasn't clear what I was fearful of. My life had taken some unexpected twists and turns lately and I was left to sort it out…or at least I hoped I could.

Chapter 5
Strange Day (By the Minutes)

A crackling snap of thunder rudely jolted me straight out of dreamy slumber. Electrical storms were a thrill for me, but not at 5:52 a.m. on a Monday. I valued sleeping in more than anything. In a few weeks, I'd once again be back to a routine of waking up at 6:05 a.m., before forcing myself into the shower ten minutes later. I wasn't especially pumped about seventh grade since receiving the news that Brinn and I only had math and English together.

Brinn kept it positive with her bright reminders, "Yeah, but we'll have cheer practice two or three evenings a week WHEN you make the Comets."

The rain pelted against my windows in huge sheets. It was useless to try to get back to sleep. I grabbed my iPod, turned up the music, and cozied up with my favorite fuzzy pink blanket. I continued to analyze how I would juggle the next level of cheer, my increasingly difficult class work, and most importantly hang out time with Brinn.

The previous cheer season had been jam-packed, and life became crazy at times. By the time I got home there was barely time for dinner and homework. I'd turn 'snarly'—that's what Mom called it when, according to her, "I was mad at the world and everyone in it."

There were a few incidents when I stomped upstairs, slammed my bedroom door as hard as possible (for grand effect), then cuddled up in my blanket to stew. After that, I only wished I could go back downstairs for a snack. Jess frequently referred to me as Oscar the Grouch, which never failed to irritate me more. Having two little sisters with nothing in common with me was irritating in general. In my make-believe world, I was an awesome only child who never had to share anything, baby sit, or listen to whiny, squeaky voices.

Then, out of nowhere, Alex showed up in my head. I was a tiny bit miffed because I hadn't contrived to think about him. But since he was there, I contemplated whether he would be in any of my classes. Then, my thoughts trailed on to the recollection of him plowing so fast through his ice cream Explosion that he acquired a "brain freeze".

It sent him squeezing his head with his hands, crying out, "AAH, OH, stupid me!"

And I don't think I was laughing AT him as

he accused. It was his theatrics that was so darn funny.

"Get out of my head, Alex. Get out, get out, get out! I have important issues to deal with," I commanded.

I had a worrisome feeling creeping in about cheer try-outs and concentrating on the big goal kept getting interrupted. I was starting to feel discombobulated, and that's not a good thing. That was one of Brinn's words for anytime she was baffled about some cheer judge's score or confused about some drama among the girls on her team. She sometimes substituted it with the word, 'bamboozled'. Well, this was where I was living, in the land of Bamboozieville.

The storm quickly passed and the sun began to stream in streaks through the trees. I opened my window to suck in a deep breath. I loved how after the rain, the wet soil and grass combine with moisture in the air to produce a damp, earthy scent. The outdoors brought a calmness that mystified and enchanted me. I held secret visions of exploring Florida State Parks to collect snapshots to create a *Snazzy, Jazzy Nature Guide for Kids*.

Every summer, our family visited a new place. I was especially drawn to the ones that offered camping and tirelessly sought ways to talk Mom and Dad into trying it. But Mom always had the same response: "That's the last thing I want to do for a vacation." She was steadfast about certain aspects of life and I doubted I'd ever change her mind.

As I stood at the window, soaking in the warmth of the sunshine, my eyes opened to see the Davis's SUV pull out of the driveway. "Great," I muttered, imagining they probably witnessed me standing there, and now perceived it as spying on them. "Ugh!" This day was off to a peculiar start.

My phone read: 7:02 a.m. At 10:15 a.m., Brinn texted to see if Mom could drop me off at just after Noon. It wasn't that Mom couldn't, it's that there was a distressful feeling tumbling around in my body. I did entirely want to go to Brinn's to see all her new clothes from the shopping spree. But, my enthusiasm for practicing drills was sinking. In fact, the motivation for gymnastics was sinking like a rock.

I fantasized about staying home to take pictures of flowers and birds. It was a crazy notion. Everything was out of sync. I wandered around my room in circles for fifteen minutes trying to pull my scattered self together. What was going on with me? Making the Galaxy Comets had been my goal—my dream, for two years. And now, less than two weeks before try-outs, I was freaked out. All was not settled in my world.

I went downstairs and Mom was in the kitchen. "I think I'm coming down with the flu, or something," I said, in a hushed, low voice. She dove into her feeling the forehead, checking my throat glands, and asking a million questions mode. I was hoping she'd order me to stay at home. But she instead placed the decision in my hands.

I hadn't missed a cheer practice or class in months. In cheer season everyone has to make it a top priority to be present unless you're on your deathbed because we practice our routines as a team. I mulled it over and wrestled between what I wanted to do and what I was expected to choose.

After obsessing for thirty-five minutes, I sent a text to Brinn explaining that I wasn't feeling well, so I'd stop over only to visit. I would go to the gym, however, because I really couldn't afford to miss any practice time at this stage of the game.

***

Brinn purchased some cool new jeans with sparkly sequins on the back pockets, two pairs of leggings in colorful pattern-prints, three sweet T-shirts (that were on clearance), and a funky denim jacket with random holes and tattered cuffs in all the right places. She tried everything on so we could vote on the First Day of School outfit.

"I love everything!" I told her. "But, my vote is for the jeans with the light blue baseball hoodie."

"That's what I was thinking, too!" Brinn quipped. We were almost always on the same page. Brinn had the most organized closet of any of our friends; with the colors and styles in specific groupings. Her clothes were trendy and flashy, plus she hit the mother-lode with hand-me-downs from her two sisters.

She had thirty-two pairs of various flip flops, flats, sandals, boots, and cheer shoes. We sorted through her skirts and dresses, a few she no longer cared for, because in her words, "They're so sixth grade!"

Later, we made macaroni and cheese, listened to music, checked out new clothes styles online, and discussed our class schedule. It was great just chillin' out for a change. At 3:30 p.m. Marla passed by Brinn's bedroom door and after a few soft knocks, enthusiastically said, "Start getting ready girls; time to hit the mats!"

The carefree, fun afternoon had sped by way too quickly.

✷✷✷

As the girls gathered at the gym, there was a noticeable, vibrant, electric energy exuding from everyone…everyone but me. Even Brinn was bubbling over more than usual. They all exchanged the latest updates in their lives (as if we hadn't seen each other all summer). While we stretched, there was a buzz of conversations, but I didn't join in with my input about back-handsprings or round offs.

During the session, I performed the stunts fairly easily, gaining support and encouragement from the others, and Brinn's, "Way to bring it, Kenz!" Unfortunately, only half of me was engaged in the moment. My body was going through the motions like a robot, but the inner 'me' seemed to have left the building.

When our session ended, I soaked in the ambiance surrounding me. Other classes were stretching, tumbling, dancing, and laughing. It was a place that was like a second home to many of the girls. Some had been in gymnastics since they were four years old.

Brinn finished reorganizing her gym bag, which always contained extra gym clothes, makeup, toothbrush, and her prized salon hairbrush she'd won in a recent fund-raising raffle. "Ready to Roll!" she exclaimed, springing from the floor with a burst of new energy.

Then, putting her arm around my shoulder, quickly added, "Uh, Kenz, why are you just standing here staring at the practice floor? Are you okay?"

"Yeah, I guess, I'm just a little … tired."

I wished for happiness to come flooding back into me, but instead, there was a sadness. Brinn clung to my arm and guided me out the gym door.

"Man, you're falling apart. We better give our BEST reasons to convince Mom to make a drive-thru run for a flurry," she adamantly suggested. We lobbied to stop to get them several times a week. The fast food ones weren't as good as Sweet Treats, but they still made us happy.

It was 6:28 p.m. when I arrived home. My family was out on the deck with dinner in progress. I plunked down in a patio chair and loaded my plate with Dad's Hawaiian Barbecue Chicken with grilled pineapple kabobs. But I couldn't eat.

When Mom asked how practice was and how I was feeling, I didn't know how to answer. I wasn't feeling well. My stomach was wrenching and knotted, but I wasn't ill. I pushed the corn around on my plate while formulating a good presentation on the subject of "me".

"Makenzie…yoo whoo? Are you okay? How was the class?" Mom asked.

"I, umm, I think…"

The brothers caught my attention. They'd

thrown a miniature soccer ball for Blake that after retrieving it, sent him furiously running in mad circles around the yard.

Blake skillfully avoided being captured by them as they laughed and shouted, "We're gonna get you, Blake, we're gonna get you!" But Blake outsmarted them and dodged their lunges as Alex plummeted to the ground in defeat.

I smiled.

"Hello, young lady, how was the class?" Mom repeated, this time with a bit of concern.

I put down my fork, cleared my throat, and with all the positivity I could find on short notice, let the words rush out, "I don't want to try out for The Comets!"

It was utter silence. Even Jess and Morgan looked stunned.

"Honey, what happened?" Mom asked as she put down her fork to learn the reason for this seemingly drastic revelation.

How could I explain this to anyone? It didn't even make sense to me. It was like a switch in my life had been turned off, and then another switch was turned on. I went over the past weeks as best as I could communicate it. I could tell they were skeptical. A lot of, Uhh huhs and, Hmmms.

They didn't believe my decision was made from a sound mind and insisted something drastically wrong must've happened that caused my sudden change of heart. And Dad interjected comments, like, "You can't just hastily quit something you've committed to."

But I wasn't hearing all of it. My thoughts were fuzzy and my mind was in reeling mode. Mom's final assessment was that I probably was justifiably nervous. Then, she shared some positive quotes designed to persuade me to go to tryouts where everyone was confident I would make the team and finally be alongside Brinn.

"Well, I didn't just start thinking about this five minutes, ago," I said, quietly. It was the hardest decision I'd ever made. A wave of relief swept over me, momentarily, and excitement started building for what seventh grade might be like without cheer consuming most of my free time. Of course, then the most horrifying thought was how to tell Brinn.

Mom urged me to sleep on it, and think about it all from a "fresh perspective in the morning." But it's all I'd thought about over the past three weeks. I decided to tell Brinn first thing in the morning. I had to.

I sat by my window searching the night sky and whispered a prayer for God's help. This was beyond me, or my courage level. I know you're not supposed to only pray to God when you need help, but I believed God was glad I asked.

It had been a long, bizarre day.

Chapter 6
Missing Oreo Flurries (and Other Things)

I, for the life of me, couldn't fall asleep. I tossed and turned, then tossed and turned some more. My mind rehearsed scenarios for telling Brinn, "The Big News". Should I go with a cheerful, sunny disposition? "Hey, my BFF and most wonderful person I know, I have something important to tell you about myself!" *Okay, that's lame.*

So, maybe I should be more somber and sad. No, because I wasn't sad. Maybe I could say I badly hurt my ankle while I was practicing. No, that'd be a big lie too easy to reveal. It was useless, I wasn't coming up with anything that sounded right.

My nervousness level skyrocketed with each passing hour. Then, I'd reflect full circle and convince myself of the fact, Brinn was my best friend. I told her everything, and this was just another thing. "You've got to get your bold on, that's all there is to it!"

I cheered myself on, swiping through photos of the two of us that took up tons of space on my phone. I knew that she cherished her sleep time, and there might be a rant session if I woke her up too early.

I waited until 9 a.m., and then bulked up my braveness.

HEY SLEEPY HEAD R U UP? 😆

A few minutes passed. I continued contemplating options.

AM NOW... 😆 *ANNOYING GIRL*
CAN YOU COME OVER RIGHT NOW?
WHY? BECAUSE OF THE BOYZ??
NOOOO!

I was nearing the point of jumping off the high dive, and it was scary up there.

***

I waited on the front step while scouring through my phone for online bargains. I schemed that I might be able to snag another pair of jeans before school started, now that Mom would save money not having to support cheer. When Marla pulled up to the curb, out popped Brinn with her beautiful smile and orange cheer bag.

"I brought my stuff. I assume we're practicing here today, but those boys better not bother you!" she said, as she hit me with her bag.

"Nah, they don't bother me anymore."

But, little did Brinn know, we weren't going to be practicing. I needed to get to the deed of announcing it. My heart nearly burst out of my chest. Mom glanced at me as we headed upstairs. She had an aura of concern and disappointment wrapped into one. She had feverishly attempted to talk me in to wait a few days before making such a drastic move.

Mom even puts forth her best digging effort to get me to uncover some possible details I may have been hiding. She tried hard to convince me to rethink it all; so much so that it came close to forcing me to go to practice. In her mind, if I practiced, and enjoyed it, then it would prove I had just experienced a fluky bad day. Case closed.

There was something wrong. I no longer wanted to try out for the cheer All-Star team. It was as simple as that.

Brinn plopped down on my bed. "You're acting kinda weird," she said.

"I have to tell you something," I whispered, sitting close beside her.

Her eyes turned large and serious like she expected me to tell her that my parents were getting a divorce. When we were ten, I had been sitting on her bed as she fought back tears and explained that her parents were splitting up. We sat there that day holding each other tightly, with me at a loss for any words to cheer her up. After that experience, Brinn lost her smile and joyous spark for the longest time. From that moment on, the gym was her "happy place."

I grabbed her hand and let the words fall out, "I'm not going to the tryouts."

"What in the world are you talking about? Have you lost your mind?"

Again, I found myself trying to explain the events that led to this shocking revelation in a way that made sense. But I could tell I wasn't getting through to her.

"I know this probably is a big surprise, but I've given it A LOT of thought, lately."

"Surprise isn't exactly the word I'd choose for this," she replied, with a blankness resonating from her face.

She walked back and forth in front of me spewing out the same line of questions as Mom had earlier. But she also infused accusations, "This is because of Alex and Nick, isn't it? I mean ever since they moved next door you've been all riled and mixed up!"

"Well, it might *look* like it has something to do with the boys moving here, but it's not because of them I want to leave cheer. It's because of me." I stared at her, hoping for a sign of acceptance.

For half an hour, we went back and forth, each representing our side with the same points over and over again. She used several approaches to woo me to go to practice, with the premise that I was simply getting jittery. She said I only needed to hang in there and use every ounce of confidence I had, and some of hers, too.

"Brinn, I, uhm…I'm learning some things about myself I never knew, and I'd like to try some new things that maybe I'll like more than cheer," I said, determined to stand tall.

"Ohhh, lemme guess—soccer!"

"Well, I do think it's fun, and I'm surprisingly pretty good at it. Look, I think I just need a little time off from cheer. I mean, I don't know, maybe I'll…."

"You know you can't take time off, Makenzie!" Her aggravation was evident. "If you do, we'll for darn sure never be on the same dream team, ever!" Brinn picked up the photo on my dresser. "We were so cute," she said disheartened, and so past tense.

I hoped my explanation would begin to sink in and she'd wrap her arms around me and assure me that everything was going to be, "A–Okay", like she often did.

"I was hoping you'd understand," I stammered.

"I don't understand! It's like I don't even know who you are anymore. Seriously, Kenzie, ever since Alex and Nick moved in you've changed. It feels like you just punched me in the stomach!"

I felt the same way.

Immediately she snatched her phone from her back pocket and began texting her mom at record speed:

MY THROAT HURTS
PICK ME UP ASAP…PLEASE!

"Brinn, I know that we…"

"I'm not talking about this anymore," Brinn snapped. "And do you still have my white sweatshirt, you know, the one with the pink hearts on it? Because, well, I'd kinda like it back".

"Oh, okay, I'll get." I couldn't fully grasp what was transpiring. In all the rehearsing I'd done, I thought that Brinn would probably be a little bummed, but I never anticipated she'd be this mad. This MAD at ME! The heaviness in the room was closing in as I offered her the sweatshirt. Brinn let me borrow it a few months back when we were heading to the beach one cool day.

"Thank you," she said, rather condescendingly.

You're not welcome!

"I'll just wait outside," she reported, as she picked up her cheer bag and walked out of my room, leaving me searching to think of just what I could've done, or should've done differently.

I followed her to the door wanting to scream, "Please try to understand!" But no words came out.

Mom came from the kitchen. "I take it Brinn's

quite upset?"

"Yep."

"Well, she probably just needs some time to work through her feelings."

"Not helping, Mom!"

From the front room window, I watched her and Marla drive down the street and out of view. A little piece of me left with her.

***

I lie in bed listening to songs from my gymnastics play list. Suddenly, a weight seemed to crush on my chest and body. It was hard to breathe, and I envisioned this must be how it feels to get caught in a big surf wave, and left to struggle to make it back up to the surface. Earlier, I had been pretty positive that this was the choice I wanted to make, but it sure didn't return any happiness to my spirit.

In all the uncertain moments I'd ever experienced at cheer or at school, the feeling that I'd just lost my best friend was terrifying. I frantically wanted to swim out of the mammoth wave and return to calm.

Mom reluctantly contacted my gymnastics instructor. I don't know what she said, but later that evening, I received some texts from a few of the other girls that simply read: **R U OK?**

I wanted to text back: ***NOT REALLY.*** But I didn't answer anyone. Nothing came from Brinn.

Mom tried to be helpful and encouraged me to text Brinn. I didn't want to (a feeling I never thought I would have when it came to Brinn). I kept questioning why couldn't she just be happy for me?

It was obvious my parents didn't quite know how to react, so they decided an after-dinner trip to Sweet Treats would be a diversion. The ice cream was absolutely no remedy, but they insisted I come along. I didn't win many battles that would go against "precious family-time", so I unwilling climbed in the back of the Jeep with my two super excited sisters who were oblivious to my pain.

Once there, I found a quiet bench out by the bay to be alone. My sisters were too bubbly, and my parents were overly positive that "friend troubles" eventually blow over. But the reality was, no one was going to snap their fingers to make Brinn understand me, or my decision.

I was not a naïve little kid. I now understood complicated situations for what they were. When Mr. Davis told me to build up my faith to conquer my fear of trying something new (like soccer), maybe he was talking about building up my faith to conquer the fear of ALL the changes that invariably come in life. I was changing, and so was my world, as I knew it. But, I liked the Makenzie I was becoming.

Still, a part of me wanted to run back to the gym to see if it wasn't too late to still try out. I scooped up a spoonful of Oreo Flurry. "Yuck, I should get my money back." My mind flashed back to the hundreds of flurries I'd had. Most had been with Brinn on the way home from the gym, or after a day practicing cartwheels and cheer stunts at the beach.

Mom sat next to me and put her arm around my shoulder. She kissed the top of my head and the floodgate burst opened. Tears began to stream down my face until my cheeks were soaked. She didn't say anything; she quietly sat watching the sparkling water.

Back in the Jeep, I checked my phone. A message from Kara, a girl from cheer, read:

ARE U OK???

NO. NO I'M NOT! I wanted to text back, but didn't want to have to explain everything.

I scrolled through my Instagram. There was Brinn making a silly face with Chelsea. I didn't validate it with a heart Emoji because I didn't "love it". As I listened to my favorite songs on my iPod, my mind drifted. *Would I possibly like the Peanut Butter Explosion?*

Day two without Brinn had me limping along at a snail's pace. Mom prompted me to stay busy because constantly thinking about Brinn would tear me up inside. Well, it was too late for that, I was already torn up. It did help keep my mind off the "situation" for a few minutes at a time when I sorted through my closet to match jeans and tops for the first week of school. But it wasn't fun without Brinn's fashion expertise.

After dinner, Mom sent me to her garden to pick a bouquet to drop off to a neighbor. *Gosh, when would the day arrive that Jess would be depended on to do this?* As I moped, I saw Alex and Nick in their backyard kicking goal shots. They saw me arranging the flowers and sprinted over to inspect my work.

"Where've you been lately?" Alex said juggling the soccer ball from knee to knee.

"Guys, I saw you, like, two days ago."

"Well, we usually see you every day, even if it's when you're leaving with Brinn," Nick said with a smirk.

So they were spying on me now?

Alex changed the subject and complained how hot and starved he was. He felt a trip to Sweet Treats was the least his parents could do after making them move and all.

"Do you want to come?" he said, as an extra bit of insurance when he asked his parents.

I hesitated, "I guess so." *What else did I have going on?*

For Real

***

Before I could deliver the flowers to the neighbor, Mrs. Davis and Mom were talking at the front door. Sweet Treat, here I come!

Mrs. Davis—Mint Chocolate Chip.

Mr. Davis—Turtle ice cream in a super-sized waffle cone.

Nick—Peanut Butter Explosion

Alex—Peanut Butter Explosion

Me—"I'll have a Peanut Butter Explosion with extra whipped cream, please," I ordered.

"What the heck? You said you didn't like peanut butter!" Alex said accusingly.

"I changed my mind, girls are allowed to do that you know." I turned my eyes toward him but not my head.

"You drive me crazy," he said, with a frown instead of his usual smirk.

"Whatever!" I said as I collected my Explosion and headed toward the patio door. "You coming?" When I glanced back at him, he simply shook his head, rolled his eyes, picked up his Explosion, and trudged toward the door with Nick sauntering behind. They immediately began to fuss again over who had more Reese's Pieces. *Oh, brother! These two competed with a relentlessness that was boggling but fiercely funny to witness.*

I dipped into my sundae, loading up a hefty

spoonful of the concoction and cautiously navigated it into my mouth. I certainly didn't want to get whipped cream all over my face. *This is ridiculously over-the-top, incredible!*

Alex interrupted my private proclamation, "What do you think of the Explosion?"

"It's alright." I shrugged my shoulders, not phased. No need for him to have cause to gloat.

Once back in the car, I made the announcement. "Just so you all know, I'm not trying out for the Galaxy Comets," I blurted it out to get it over with. Dead silence. Then came an onslaught of wild "Woo Hoos" and spirited applause.

"Okay, let's see what team you can get on," Alex said without holding back the excitement of looking up information on soccer programs in our city.

"Hey, guys, I didn't say anything about playing soccer," I claimed. Little did they know, I had already conducted my own online searches for a nearby program, but didn't have much of a clue of how to choose.

The boys continued rattling on about how good the area offerings were and sent me several links that had their stamp of excellence. They were soccer nuts, but they made me laugh. And I was truly amazed at their insane love for any food that included cheese or peanut butter.

That night, I went to bed anticipating the next

day. Mom agreed to help me check out the soccer programs—even though she wasn't 100% supportive of my decision. I smiled as I thought of how the boys counted the Reese's Pieces on their sundaes…and that Nick had five more than Alex!

My smile faded as Brinn came to mind. I checked my phone for a text I might have missed, but no Brinn. I checked my Instagram and there she was…just not with me. I lie awake for hours making a mental list of what I already missed about her and wondered if she was ever coming back.

Chapter 7
Wind in my Hair

Day four and still no Brinn. With one decision my world turned upside down. It was obvious Brinn was avoiding me, and the loneliness grew inside me more each day. I couldn't accept that she wasn't missing me. The fact she didn't ask how I was doing wounded my soul.

On day five, there was a nagging ache gnawing at my stomach. And that's when I couldn't take it another second! I had to take the scary chance of reaching out to Brinn to try to fix this big mess.

CAN YOU COME OVER AND HANG OUT?

A long hour passed before she replied:
***SORRY…SUPER BUSY…
A LOT GOING ON LATELY***

OH

I didn't add a sad face. I didn't want her to think my heart was breaking in two. She wasn't interested in spending time with me. That was glaringly clear.

When my text chirped a few minutes later, I'd hoped she had changed her mind. But it was from Alex. Their mom was taking them to The Sport Emporium to get new soccer cleats and wanted to know if I wanted to tag along. Well, they were shoe experts who could guide me to a pair for myself. Plus, I was growing pathetic wandering around the house like a miserable zombie.

I hurried to my room, slipped into a pair of comfortable ripped jeans and a T–shirt that read: **For Real.** Assessing myself in the mirror, I clipped my hair into a side ponytail and said, "Hi boys," while flashing a peace sign at my reflection.

What just happened?

***

I'm not sure why I found it stupidly hilarious when Alex put on size 13 basketball high tops and clomped around the shoe department.

"They fit perfectly," he said smiling.

Moments later, Nick tried on hot pink cleats from the women's section and Alex said in a high-pitched girly voice, "Oh, they're just SO you."

More giggling—I just couldn't help it! We traveled throughout the store rifling through the clearance racks, selecting the most outrageous running pants with wild color patterns or gaudy flowery prints for one another. At the soccer balls display, we voted for our top-pick, which left Nick pining for a new blue and green one because, according to him, "No one can have too many soccer balls." Of course, Mrs. Davis thought otherwise.

Just when I thought they couldn't possibly make me laugh harder, I was wrong. The store had one of those super-sized gumball machines where you put in a quarter and a giant gumball glides down through a series of spiral twists, shoots, and tunnels. A yellow one rolled down for me.

Alex was bummed that he got a white one. Nick put in three quarters and ended up with a blue, orange, and red one that he instantly popped in his mouth… all at the same time! We stood near the exit doors as spectacles to customers when gobs of multi-colored drool began dribbling down Nick's chin. Mrs. Davis didn't think it was as humorous.

"Go spit some of that out," she ordered. But he didn't.

On our way back home, Nick grabbed his phone and instructed us to scooch up close and open our mouths wide to reveal our ginormous gum wads and colorful tongues. He posted it for the world to see and sent a copy to my phone.

"You're a goofball," he said.

"Takes one to know one."

It had been a drastically different shopping excursion than any I had with Brinn and her sisters. Usually, we were on time and budget limits, so finding the best bargains was more of a serious mission rather than a comedy show.

★★★

I sat on my deck examining the picture of the three of us. *What a couple of dorks.* These two managed to make me laugh even when I wasn't with them!

I started getting back to life—it just was a different life. Mom received an email that I'd been placed on a community AYSO team, which was open to anyone at any experience level. That's when it sunk in. I was stepping out and taking a chance on my own!

I filled in all my practices and games on the family calendar and followed Mom around the kitchen, explaining all the soccer rules I'd learned. Still, whenever Brinn crossed my mind, a vibe ran through me and I'd whisper, "Please God, please bring her back to me."

The morning of the tryouts I woke up sadder than words can describe. It had been less than

two weeks without Brinn, but it felt like a lifetime. I sent her a text:
GOOD LUCK
Several minutes later:
THANX
I contemplated adding, **I'M SORRY**, but I still didn't know what I was sorry for. The only thing that stood out was I was sorry she was mad and extra sorry that she wasn't happy for me.

Fortunately, it was a Saturday, and I was joining the Davis clan on a morning run. The boys, their dad, and an over-joyed Blake waited for me in front of their house. I leaned down to give Blake a good morning hug, and he returned the sentiment with a big lick that glided across my cheek all the way to my lips. He fit right in the Davis family that was for sure!

There we were, the new group of people and a dog running through the neighborhood in sleek rhythm. Ah, the fresh air and sunshine. Fantastical. We passed other runners and neighbors who walked dogs or watered their plants. It felt like a tighter community of friendliness that I'd not taken much notice of before.

When we arrived back at the Davises, I snapped a photo of the four of us. Blake was in front so his nose looked huge and his tongue hung out of the corner of his mouth. Mr. Davis looked cool in his sunglasses with an arm around each boy's shoulder. Alex smirked, Nick flexed his muscles, and I tilted my head in so I could fit in the shot. Cool!

Brinn, Chelsea, and Kara made it on the Comets team (as expected). They posted their raving snapshots of jubilant faces. I congratulated all three. Brinn didn't acknowledge it. I went to bed with an empty and angry heart. School was starting in less than two weeks and I couldn't grab hold of the notion that Brinn was treating me like her enemy. I wished for a magic fairy wand to make it all go back to when she was on my side.

***

The first day of school was dreadful, just like I'd imagined. Brinn returned an obligated, "Hi," when I approached her and Chelsea in math class. Then, an awkward silence.

I chose a seat next to a girl named, Lainey, who I knew from other classes. Lainey was a good attitude kind of girl mixed with a little sassy. She was in the Nature Photography club and could literally talk for hours about dolphins. She had already determined she would become a marine biologist. I found her dreams to be downright fascinating.

In truth, I did miss being with the cheer

team, immensely. There was hardly an hour that passed that a memory about cheer-life didn't skip through my mind. But, I couldn't deny that something was brewing inside me and my premonition was that brighter days were set to come. I was super-jazzed to begin building a portfolio to highlight my unique photo flair. And my soccer savvy...I was on fire!

I had one class with Alex, Team Sports. Now, I would have the opportunity to continue proving my athletic bent. I introduced him to some classmates, but he didn't really need much help. I admit I was sort of jealous at how effortless it seemed for him to find friends.

But, I admired him, too, realizing how difficult it must be to leave all your old friends, move halfway across the country, and start seventh grade at a new school. It also was perplexing that he was the one that made me feel like I fit in.

I'd love to say things between Brinn and me improved during the week, but nothing was farther from the truth. There existed coolness in the space between us. I desperately wanted to ask her if we could sit down for a heart-to-heart to confess how we felt about what happened.

We could then agree to put our hurts in a box, bury them and never dig them up again. We could just go back to being best friends. Only if that was possible. I didn't have the nerve.

I was terrified she'd say there was nothing we needed to discuss and have to face the reality that my friendship didn't hold enough value to fight for. I couldn't bear the thought of hearing her tell me that we were no longer on the same path, or how we were clearly moving in two opposite directions.

I hung out with Lainey, Alex, and some other kids I knew from sixth grade. Every once in a while I'd spot Nick in the hallway and he'd throw out a, "Hey, Big Mak!" He typically had a group of girls hovering around him…and he loved it!

Lainey and I officially signed up for the Nature Photography Club. It was sure to be a blast from the kinds of field trips on the roster. I told Mom I should probably get a nice digital camera—or at least a phone upgrade for quality photographs.

"Oh boy, here we go again! Now it's cameras and soccer cleats!" Mom said with a sort of sarcastic tone.

It wouldn't surprise me if she was thinking, "*Wow, I'm still shoveling out the dollars, and I guess that's never going to change!*"

Then she added, "It's great seeing your smile again."

Soccer had a lot to do with it. I was placed on a coed team, and although I hadn't known anyone beforehand, my teammates welcomed me into their world from the very first practice. Since there were boys on the team, we developed a different kind of camaraderie than I had with just being with the girls at cheer.

I have to say, the boys provided a wackiness that assured there'd never be a dull practice! And thanks to the Davis Brothers Boot Camp, I really didn't seem that far behind. It's amazing what a little effort and hard work can accomplish.

It was a new life I never saw coming.

***

On Friday after school, Alex, Lainey and I planned to walk to Sweet Treat. It was declared my First Pre-Game Pump-Up Party. I didn't need a ton of pumping up in my view, but it was a good excuse for getting ice cream. Coach Brandon was astonished and pleased with the progress I'd accomplished in only a few weeks, and so was I.

At the end of the day, while collecting my books from my locker, Brinn brushed close to my back. "Good Luck", I heard her say. That was all.

I watched her stride down the hall and lost her in the sea of kids. I crossed my fingers and repeated a familiar plea, "Please come back to me."

***

I thought I'd be a crazy wreck Saturday morning, but as I arrived at the soccer field, I instead felt a whirlwind of crazy anticipation. As we sat in a large circle on the field, the eleven of us strapped on our shin guards and confirmed to each other we were going to be one stellar team!

Searching the bleachers, I hoped to see Brinn's smiling face in the crowd. To know she'd accepted my decision and supported it would mean the world to me. But she was absent.

My family, the Davises, and Lainey were my cheering section. Shuffling through my sports bag, I found the World Cup pin Alex gave me. I pinned it to the underside of my jersey (he insisted it always brought him good luck). We weren't allowed to wear pins or jewelry, but I didn't point it out to anyone and surmised that some of the others probably had their own good luck charm somewhere too.

I also brought the friendship bracelet Brinn gave me for my 10th birthday and slid it down underneath the backside of my sock. "Well, I'm taking you with me, anyway," I exclaimed. Brinn's spirit still lingered inside me. I wasn't ready to let her go.

The team huddled as Coach Brandon stated his final strategies and line-up. When he called my name for right forward, he turned to me, giving me two thumbs up!

"Good to go, Coach!" I smiled back. With the team placing their hands together in the middle of our circle we shouted with fervor, "Go Stingrays!"

Standing in kick-off position I absorbed the expense of the surrounding soccer fields. The sky reflected a brilliant blue and the trees in the distance were dancing in the breeze. Crossing my fingers, I scanned the bleachers one last time.

Maybe someday.

Time stood still for a couple seconds. Then, the whistle blew, and I was off like a bandit. I ran down the field with the wind blowing briskly through my hair. It was extraordinarily exhilarating.

I heard Alex's voice above the crowd, "Bend it like Hutchinson!"

I pretended I didn't hear him. But I did intend to go for the goal.

For Real

ABOUT THE AUTHOR

Robin Stewart earned a Bachelor of Art degree in English/Creative Writing from Western Michigan University. She launched out with a focus on business writing, but her long-held dream was to shift to creative fiction for younger readers. *For Real* is Robin's debut book.

When she isn't writing in her studio, her main interests include kayaking, sailing, hiking, walking the beach, music, concerts, and spending time with family. She and her husband divide their time between Michigan and Florida.

Robin has two married sons and five grandchildren who keep her on the go and have no problem talking her into watching kid-themed movies.